WHAT AUSTRALIAN ANIMAL AM I?

Written and Illustrated by

Jacinta Padgett

ISBN-10: 1482071649
ISBN-13: 978-1482071641

DEDICATION

For Mum and Dad – Thank you for everything.

Australia is a country of extremes. Heat waves, bushfires and flooding are just some of the harsh realities of life here.

Because of that, our native animals have had to adapt to life in a vast, challenging and unforgiving environment.

Many of the animals that live here are often not found anywhere else in the world.

But that isn't the only thing that makes them so special.

Welcome to the wonderful world of Australian animals.

How many do you know?

I use my powerful legs to bounce
through the bush.

My large tail helps me to balance.

Females have a pouch.

I am either red, or grey.

I am . . .

. . . a kangaroo.

I have long legs and a long neck.

I can run really fast.

My feathers are brown, and soft to touch.

I am a bird, but I can't fly.

I am . . .

. . . an emu.

I have soft, grey fur and large round ears.

My name is Aboriginal for 'no drink'.

I eat eucalyptus leaves.

Most of my time is spent sleeping high up in trees.

I am . . .

. . . a koala.

I am a mammal, but I hatch out of an egg.

When I swim I close my eyes.

My tail is shaped like a paddle,
and I have a duck-like bill.

Males have venomous spurs on their back feet.

I am . . .

. . . a platypus.

I use my sharp claws to burrow under the ground.

Females carry their babies in
a back-to-front pouch.

I am short, with a big tough backside.

My fur is usually grey or brown.

I am ...

. . . a wombat.

I am a bird.

I like to eat insects, snakes and mice.

My laughter echoes through the bush.

I like to live in a large family group.

I am . . .

. . . a kookaburra.

I use my long sticky tongue to catch my dinner.

My body is covered with sharp spikes.

When I'm frightened I curl up into a ball.

Just like the platypus, I am a mammal that hatches out of an egg.

I am . . .

. . . an echidna.

I sleep through the day and come out at night.

My big eyes help me to see in the dark.

I cannot fly, but I 'glide' between trees.

I have a sweet tooth.

I am . . .

. . . a sugar glider.

I am black and white.

I bang my food on the ground before I eat it.

I protect my young and my nest very fiercely.

I am often called a 'songbird'.

I am . . .

. . . a magpie.

Australian animals are unlike most other animals found throughout the world and many of them are not found anywhere else.

We can help our Australian animal friends stay healthy by making sure we know how our actions can affect them, and by doing things that help, not hurt.

This could be doing something as simple as teaching others about how the bush is an important part of our landscape. It provides shelter, and food, for many of the animals you've learnt about in this book.

Weeds can harm areas where these animals live, so by planting local species in your garden you can help protect their home.

There are lots of other things we can do as well, such as picking up rubbish and putting it in the bin (even if it is not yours), and not feeding wild animals. Food that isn't part of an animal's normal diet can hurt their tummy.

If we all do our part our Australian animal friends will thank us for it and we can help to make sure they are around for a very long time to come.

Printed in Great Britain
by Amazon